My Name is BOB

JAMES BOWEN
& GARRY JENKINS

ILLUSTRATED BY
GERALD KELLEY

RED FOX

To Kitty, Twig, Penelope, John, Sue and, always, Bob – J.B.

To Cilene, Gabriella and Tom – G.J.

For Vicki, Lucie, Kirsten & James – G.K.

MY NAME IS BOB
A RED FOX BOOK 978 1 782 95081 3

Published in Great Britain by Red Fox, an imprint of Random House Children's Publishers UK
A Random House Group Company

This edition published 2014

10 9 8 7 6 5 4 3 2 1

Red Fox Books are published by Random House Children's Publishers UK, 61–63 Uxbridge Road, London W5 5SA

www.randomhousechildrens.co.uk
www.randomhouse.co.uk

Addresses for companies within The Random House Group Limited can be found at: www.randomhouse.co.uk/offices.htm

THE RANDOM HOUSE GROUP Limited Reg. No. 954009

A CIP catalogue record for this book is available from the British Library.

Printed in China

My name is Bob
and I'm a street cat.

Shall I tell you my story?
Then come with me . . .

I wasn't always a street cat. I grew up
in a quiet house with a kind old lady.
She looked after me. She loved me and
I loved her. I would curl up in her cosiest
chair and listen to the beautiful music
she played. I thought I was the luckiest
little cat in the world.

Then one day the old lady wasn't well.
I wanted to make her better so I sat
on her lap, watching over her from
morning till night. But there was
nothing I could do to help her.

One day, some men in an ambulance came.
I hoped they could make her better,
so I chased down the road after them.

I ran and ran and tried
to keep up. I jumped on
to a bus thinking it would
follow her. But instead it
took me on a long journey
into the big city.

After a time, the driver made me jump off the bus.
The streets were busy and noisy – everybody was rushing
around so fast. "I wish I could go back home,"
I said to myself. But I didn't have a home any more.

I tried to get some food
from a dustbin, but some
street cats snarled at me.

"Get lost!" one of them spat.
I felt frightened and ran away.

I ran and ran through the
crowded streets, not knowing where I was.
That night I slid inside a cardboard box in the
doorway of a shop. It was warm and cosy and
it made me think of home. "I miss curling up
in my chair. How I miss my home," I thought.

The next morning a big man woke me up. **"Scram!"**
he shouted, shaking me out of my box. I ran away.

Days passed. Everywhere I
went, people chased me off.

Weeks passed.
I crept away and hid.

And then one morning I heard a friendly voice. "Hello, pussycat, do you want to come home with me?" "Yes please," I purred. I was so happy that someone wanted me.

But his mother wouldn't let me in. "I'm not having that smelly cat in my house," she said, and she slammed the door closed.

I stared at my reflection in a puddle. The face in the water
didn't look like me. I was so scruffy and dirty, as though I hadn't
washed for a year. I was cold and hungry and too tired even to
lick myself clean. "Will I ever find a home again?" I thought.

Day after day I walked and walked.

Nobody wanted to feed me.

Nobody wanted to take me in.

Nobody wanted to be my friend.

Winter came, but my life hadn't changed.
I was alone, hungry and cold, on the streets.

But then, when spring came, my luck changed . . .
I heard music! Beautiful music. I followed
the sound and saw a man playing his guitar.

I could tell he was sad and
lonely like me. He looked like
he needed a friend.

So I followed him home
and waited outside for him.

That night I saw a pair
of eyes glowing in the dark.
I was cornered. The creature
bit me as I tried to escape.

The next morning, my leg hurt so much
that I hobbled inside the building and sat
by the stairs. "Perhaps the man will see me here,"
I thought. "Perhaps he will help me." Then I heard . . .

"Hello, little fella.
You look hungry,"
the man said.
"Do you want to
come up for some
milk and
tuna?"

The man was kind. He stroked me gently and put medicine
on my leg. "Don't worry, you're safe with me," he said.
I felt I could trust him, he seemed like a friend. He told me
his name was James. "And I'm going to call you Bob," he said.

When my leg was better, James and I went out to play music. On the streets, people smiled and gathered to watch us: James and his street cat named Bob.

I sat at his feet while he strummed his guitar. I thought I was the luckiest little cat in the world, just like before.

From that day on
we've been together -
and we always will be.

Bob
AND
James

ABOUT JAMES AND BOB

In March 2007 James Bowen, a busker, found an injured ginger tom cat in the hallway of the North London block of flats where he lived. Realising he was a homeless stray, James gave the cat somewhere to sleep and spent most of the little money he had on medicine to heal his wounds.

He nursed the cat back to health, expecting him to return to the streets. But Bob, as James had named him, had other ideas. He started following James around, even jumping on a bus one morning as his new friend headed to work in Covent Garden.

Soon the pair had become a popular sight on the streets of London. People stopped to talk to James and give him money and presents for Bob. James had been homeless himself and was trying to make a new life. Together, he and Bob helped each other to find happiness and hope again.

In 2012 *A Street Cat Named Bob*, a book about their adventures, written by James with my help, was published. It became a best-seller around the world. Today, the pair still live together in London, where they are working on more books and raise money for charities that help animals and the homeless. There are plans to turn their story into a movie.

Garry Jenkins

London, 2013